To my Bugvillian family and the 'RoolaBoola' children of Castlebar.

Paul Howard is a very successful illustrator whose illustrations for the picture book of *The Owl Who was Afraid of the Dark* by Jill Tomlinson have been widely acclaimed. Paul lives in Belfast with his wife and three children. *Bugville* is the first book Paul has written.

and now it's time for ...

BUGVILLE

Written and illustrated
by Paul Howard

EGMONT

EGMONT
We bring stories to life

Bugville first published in Great Britain 2012
by Egmont UK Limited
239 Kensington High Street
London W8 6SA

Text and illustrations copyright © 2012 Paul Howard

The moral rights of the author have been asserted

ISBN 978 1 4052 4925 6

1 3 5 7 9 10 8 6 4 2

A CIP catalogue record for this title is available
from the British Library

Printed and bound in Great Britain by the CPI Group (UK) Ltd, Croydon, CR0 4YY

46678/1

EGMONT

Our story began over a century ago, when seventeen-year-old
Egmont Harald Petersen found a coin in the street. He was on
his way to buy a flyswatter, a small hand-operated printing
machine that he then set up in his tiny apartment.

The coin brought him such good luck that today Egmont has
offices in over 30 countries around the world. And that lucky
coin is still kept at the company's head offices in Denmark.

MIX
Paper
FSC® C018306

CONTENTS

This is Bugville.

One mighty fine city.

Dozens of zoos and gardens.

Scores of theatres and museums.

Hundreds of burger bars.

Thousands of fancy-dress-hire stores.

And millions of …

BUGS!

Bugs that included two *extraordinary* flies – a housefly called Superfly and a midge called, er, Midge.

They were Bugville's very own superheroes. Why, everyone loved those flies!

Superfly and Midge didn't like to talk about themselves or their adventures. But they'd certainly made Bugville a safer place, putting plenty of bad bugs behind bars. Well, OK, so there were still a few crazy bugs out there causing trouble, like…

AAAAAAAARRGGHHHHH!!
Look up there!

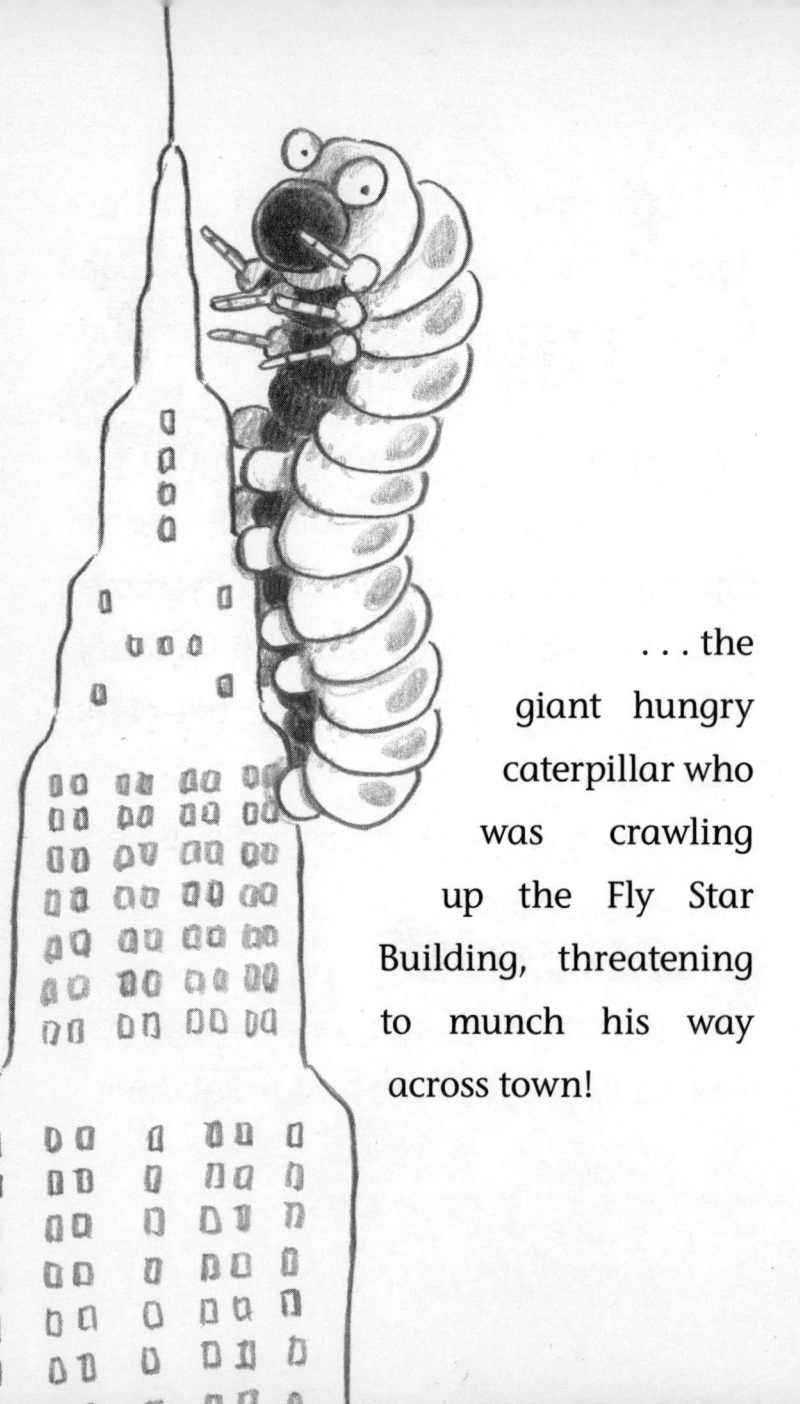

. . . the giant hungry caterpillar who was crawling up the Fly Star Building, threatening to munch his way across town!

Chapter 1
SUPERFLY!

Superfly and Midge were already there, ready to save the day. Midge did a fancy back-flip in the air and faced the giant caterpillar.

'Look out, Midge!' Superfly yelled. 'He's got goo guns!'

PEEEOOOWWW!

The caterpillar shot goo at Midge and crawled further up the Fly Star Building.

But wait! It wasn't a real caterpillar.

It was a giant ROBOTIC caterpillar with goo guns instead of legs.

The caterpillar climbed up the mast on the top of the building . . .

BOOIIIIIIIN

. . . and was flung into the air.

Midge had pulled the mast back, then let it go. What a mighty midge!

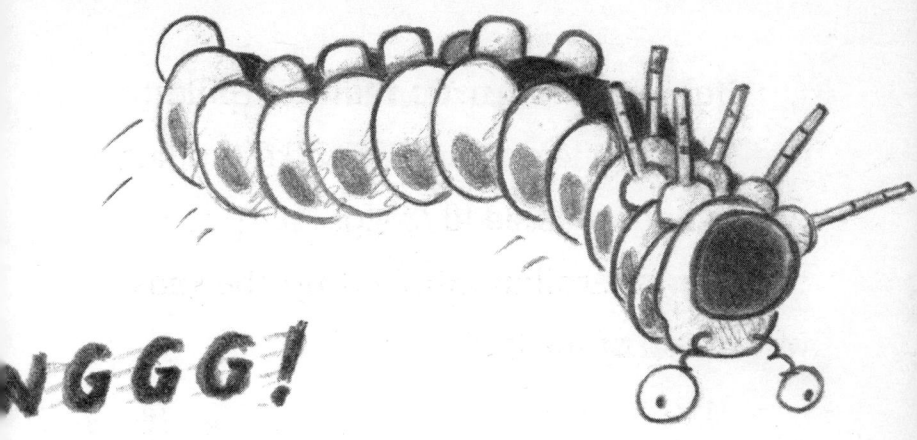

NGGG!

GRASH!

The caterpillar landed on the roof of the Bugville Art Museum. His goo guns drooped. His big head slumped. He was **5...4...3...2...1...OUT!** But then, after the silence, there was a hissing noise. And ... *sniff* ... a disgusting smell!

Ugh! It was the caterpillar! The rotten leaf-muncher was spraying stink gas!

Midge revealed his razor-sharp teeth and started snapping at the air. What was he going to do now?

At a quick nod from Superfly, the incredible midge flew down and began chomping his way around the edge of the museum's glass dome to loosen it from the roof. Then, with Superfly's help, he lifted the heavy dome and dropped it over the caterpillar, trapping it and its stinky gas inside.

Thick gas filled the dome, making the caterpillar hard to see. The gathering

crowds pushed forward for a closer look, when, suddenly, a hatch opened in the caterpillar's head.

Then something stepped out of the caterpillar on to the roof! Who on earth could it be?

'It's Nasty Nat!' said Superfly. 'The nastiest gnat in Bugville.'

Nasty Nat? He was supposed to be in jail!

'Quick, Midge, cut a hole in the glass,' said Superfly.

The heroes dragged Nasty Nat out and handed him to the police.

Superfly and Midge. The city's favourite heroes. They'd saved Bugville – *again.*

Within seconds, the boys were surrounded by news reporters, all yelling questions.

Aah, poor Midge. They didn't ask him anything! Not to worry, Superfly didn't answer them anyway. He'd turned to face the crowds. All of Bugville waited, party poppers held high, mouths open to sing. They were waiting to hear Superfly yell three words. The three words he always said. Three little words that told them Bugville was safe once again.

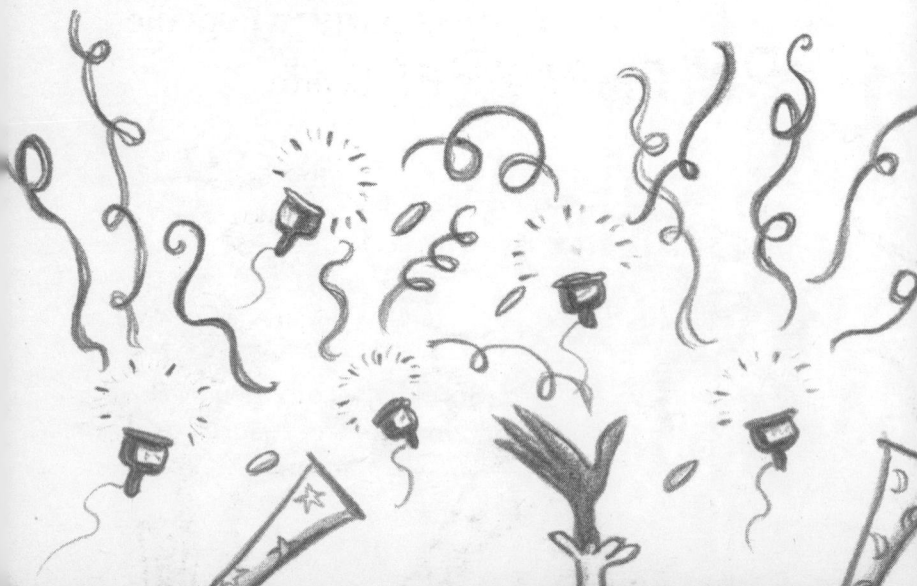

'PIECE O' CAKE!'

... and then - **P^OP!** -

the biggest - **P^OP!** -

street party in Bugville

P^OP! P^OP! P^OP! began.

Chapter 2
BUUURP!

Across town, in Scrappy Burgers, the grubbiest burger bar in Bugville, chilli dippers were flying out of the kitchen.

More dippers on table nine.

Fleas–burger on ten, wings on the side.

'Come on, make it snappy back there,' Mr Scrappy hollered. 'This is *fast* food, remember?' The bossy dog-flea flicked **Fly News** on to the TV.

'Hey – Superfly and Midge are on!'

Mr Scrappy loved Superfly and Midge. Unfortunately, his customers . . .

. . . didn't. They preferred Bugville the way it had been – a rotten, crime-ridden city that stank of stale underpants. Yuck!

Well, on that miserable night, the mean-looking slug at table five wasn't happy either. He'd had enough of Superfly and Midge too. Only *he* planned on doing something about it.

BUUUUURRRPPP!

'Waiter!' the gross slug bellowed. 'Get me more onion wings!' The slug's voice dropped to a low tremor. 'Get me Superfly and that ridiculous Midge – on toast!'

'Oh!' said the waiter, a creepy woodlouse. He glanced over at Mr Scrappy, who was cleaning the TV. 'You no like Bugville's heroes, eh?'

'NO!' the slug spat. 'I detest flies! I detest all flies! But most of all, I detest Superfly! *"Piece o' cake, Piece o' cake."* What kind of a stupid catchphrase is that?'

Sparks shot out of the slug, hitting

the lightshade and setting the waiter's notepad on fire.

Who was this sparking slug?

Who was this lightning-shooting meanie?

It was . . .

15

...**ELECTRO SLUG**! The slimiest slug in town. One big, bad boy who, years before, had left Bugville to escape from all the flies. Now he was back.

The frazzled waiter moved closer. 'You no like Superfly and Midge, eh?' he said, narrowing his eyes. 'Well . . .' He shuffled closer. 'Me no like them either.'

'Fabulous!' the slug erupted. 'Take a seat, Mr . . . ?'

'Oh! Everyone call me Loo.'

'Loo? As in . . . ?'

'Yes. Loo – same thing as toilet.'

'Well, Mr . . . er . . . Loo. You dislike Superfly and Midge . . . I detest them. Maybe we can help each other?'

Two hours went by. Two hours full of sinister cackles, litres of pop and several trips to the stinking bathroom.

Two hours spent:

1. Not waiting tables.

2. Electrifying Mr Scrappy, the boss.

3. Watching customers leave.

AAAAAARRGGHHH!!

and 4. Finishing everyone's leftovers.

Until, long after their bed-time, Electro Slug and Loo had finally come up with a cunning, evil plan!

Chapter 3

NO PAIN, NO GAIN

Whenever Superfly and Midge weren't saving bugs, they'd be busy signing autographs, helping charities or doing everyday things like visiting the City Library and Alder's Lice-Cream Parlour. Or, like most mornings, they'd be going for their daily work-out at the gym. They did have to be super-fit to beat all those bad bugs after all!

Buff-Tips Gym was where Bugville's footballers, tennis players and tiddly-wink champions worked out. Regulars included Stag Taggart – Bugville's number one wrestling stag beetle – and, of course, Superfly and Midge.

That particular morning, the boys were meeting their new trainer.

'I'm gonna work you two hard,' the scary beetle barked.

'I'm gonna make you boys sweat. You gonna sweat from places you ain't ever sweat from before!'

Yes, he was tough.

'No pain, no gain. You gotta work to look good!'

Superfly nodded. 'Well we do want to look good for the Bugville TV Awards tonight, Midge.' Then he spotted the new trainer's name badge. 'Right? *Wally.*'

'Hehehehehehehe,' Midge sniggered.

'Smart fly, huh? Drop and give me fifty press-ups!' Wally snarled. 'NOW!'

Yes, he really was tough.

Tough and no fun!

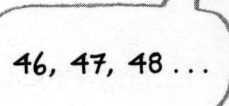

46, 47, 48 . . .

'Now, let's see you funny flies run.'

'OK,' Superfly gasped, 'WALLY.'

The trainer set the running machine at top speed.

'Sit-ups!' yelled Wally. 'Kick-boxing!'

'Rowing machine!' the beefy bug bellowed. Then finally . . . 'Weights!'

Wally lay back to prepare to lift a terrifyingly heavy bar.

'I can't wait to see Freya Lemar at the Awards tonight, Midge,' Superfly panted, winking at Midge before he slipped a few more weights on to Wally's bar. 'You know – the **Fly News** reporter.'

Midge jokingly blew his pal a kiss and added more weights on the other side of the bar. What were those two up to?

'Well, I think she deserves an award,'

Superfly concluded as the two mischievous friends kicked the supporting stands away!

Midge stretched and yawned.

'You worn out, buddy?' Superfly said. 'Come on. Let's hit the showers.'

Wally couldn't hold the heavy bar any longer. Finally it fell, trapping him underneath.

'HEY!' Wally bellowed. 'Quit your chitter-chatter and get this weight off me – NOW!'

But the heroes were distracted. Superfly's antennae were vibrating. His phone was ringing. The hero lifted the phone off his weapons belt. An old grasshopper appeared on the mini-screen.

'Young one,' the grasshopper began.

'Yes, Grand Master?' said Superfly.

'I've just had a vision,' the grasshopper said.

'Again, Grand Master?' Superfly asked.

'Yes,' the grasshopper confirmed. 'And I saw your future.'

Midge rolled his eyes. Grand Master Grasshopper was always predicting the future.

'Really?' Superfly said, acting surprised.

'Yes! Come quickly. I need to tell you about it. Before it is too late.' The old grasshopper sounded worried. 'Oh, and young one . . .'

'Yes, Grand Master?' said Superfly.

'Pick up some lunch on your way.'

Chapter 4

FANCY'S DEPARTMENT STORE

Along the street from Buff-Tips, a taxi cab pulled up. Out jumped the most gorgeous blue-bottle – Freya Lemar – the news reporter Superfly had been wondering about.

Fly Weekly – Bugville's juiciest gossip magazine – had been running stories about Freya and Superfly 'dating' for weeks. But it was only gossip, of course. They hardly even knew each other!

Freya headed into Fancy's – Bugville's finest department store. Her hornet workmate, Melba Modem, joined her in the revolving door.

'Make this the last store, honey,' Melba moaned. 'My shoes are startin' to rub.'

'Sorry, Melba,' Freya apologised. 'I didn't think finding a dress for the Bugville TV Awards would be this tough.'

'Oh, don't apologise, honey,' Melba said, accepting a free spray of perfume. 'You're sure to find the perfect dress here. This store's full of surprises. Besides, you deserve to win that Award tonight. You're the best news reporter in Bugville.'

They went up to the ladies' fashion department.

'Try that rail of dresses over there,' Melba said. 'I'll start right here.'

Freya had just begun to look through the dresses when . . .

. . . a blubbery slug poked his head out from behind the clothes rail.

'Oh, Miss Lemar! You are so beautiful and talented,' he gushed. 'Please sign an autograph for my friend here.'

The startled reporter looked down to see a greasy woodlouse grinning up at her.

'We your biggest fans, Miss Lemar,' the woodlouse added, pushing a grubby notepad in her face. She frantically scribbled her name and handed the pad back.

'Thank you, Miss Lemar,' the slug nodded, as he and his pal slipped away. 'This is very . . . useful.'

It was the two creeps from Scrappy Burgers – **Electro Slug** and the waiter, Loo. They were up to something. And it was bound to be no good.

BBBRRRRIIINNNGGG!!!

Freya's phone started ringing in her bag.

BBBBRRRRIIIINNNNGGGG!!!!!!

She tipped the bag up and everything fell out. She grabbed the phone. 'Freya Lemar speaking,' she said. 'Oh, Amy. Hi!'

Melba rushed over. 'Don't worry, honey, I'll get these,' she whispered, bending down to lift Freya's belongings off the floor.

One by one, she put everything back in the bag: a postcard from Hambug ... some Fly-dent chewing gum ... her gym pass ... wig-tape ... a note from Superfly ...

To Bugville's favourite news reporter —

Superfly

P.S. You're my favourite too!
X

her perfume ... some dental floss ... some airline tickets . . . her purse . . . pens . . . an old lottery ticket . . . her nail file . . . a clip-on microphone . . . her diary . . . and lastly, a photo of Superfly . . .

'Melba!' Freya cried once her phone call was over.

'Coming, honey,' her friend replied, lifting Freya's bag. But just then she saw a dress she liked and got sidetracked.

'Melba, quick!' Freya called. 'I think I've found the dress.' The reporter spun around just as Melba finally arrived. 'How do I look?'

Melba Modem stood in silence – a rare thing. 'Beautiful, honey,' she sighed. 'Just beautiful.'

BBBBBBRRRRRIIIIIIIINNNNGGGGG!!!!!

Freya's phone rang from the changing room.

'Hello, Freya Lemar,' she said, breathlessly. As she listened to the voice on the other end of the line, Freya's face turned pale.

'What's the matter, honey?' asked Melba, arriving as Freya ended the call.

'Something bad's going on at Turnbull's Fancy-Dress-Hire Store,' Freya said. 'They need a reporter over there – now!'

Chapter 5
ROOM OF GLOOM

On the 81st floor of Tick Towers, in Grand Master's apartment, Superfly and Midge were finishing their sushi. Grand Master Grasshopper had insisted on eating before telling them about his vision.

Although he was blind, the old grasshopper had 'visions'. Unfortunately, they were full of doom. Especially the ones about Bugville.

Superfly and Midge were quite used to the grasshopper's gloomy visions – they had been his students since they were maggots in Bluey Bottle's Circus. It was Grand Master who had taught them how to be superheroes.

After Superfly and Midge had told their tutor about how they had saved a ladybug from a runaway shopping trolley, they followed the glum grasshopper out of the kitchen.

Scented candles lit the room. Oriental music played in the background. Grand Master sat down among the candles. His head swayed for a while until, finally, he spoke.

'I sense a difference in you today, young one.'

Superfly and Midge gazed nervously at each other. Grand Master had 'seen' what was on their minds. But which one of them was he talking about?

'There is a lightness in your heart. There is someone you like very much.'

Midge sighed. Superfly gulped. The grasshopper was talking about him!

'There is nowhere to hide,' Grand Master reminded him. 'These feelings will distract you. You must remain focused – the time is near. The time when evil forces will surround you. A time you will need to search deep within yourself to win. My vision showed me all this. Your feelings will . . . **BWERRR!**'

The grasshopper's head jerked back suddenly, as if he'd been hit with a frying pan.

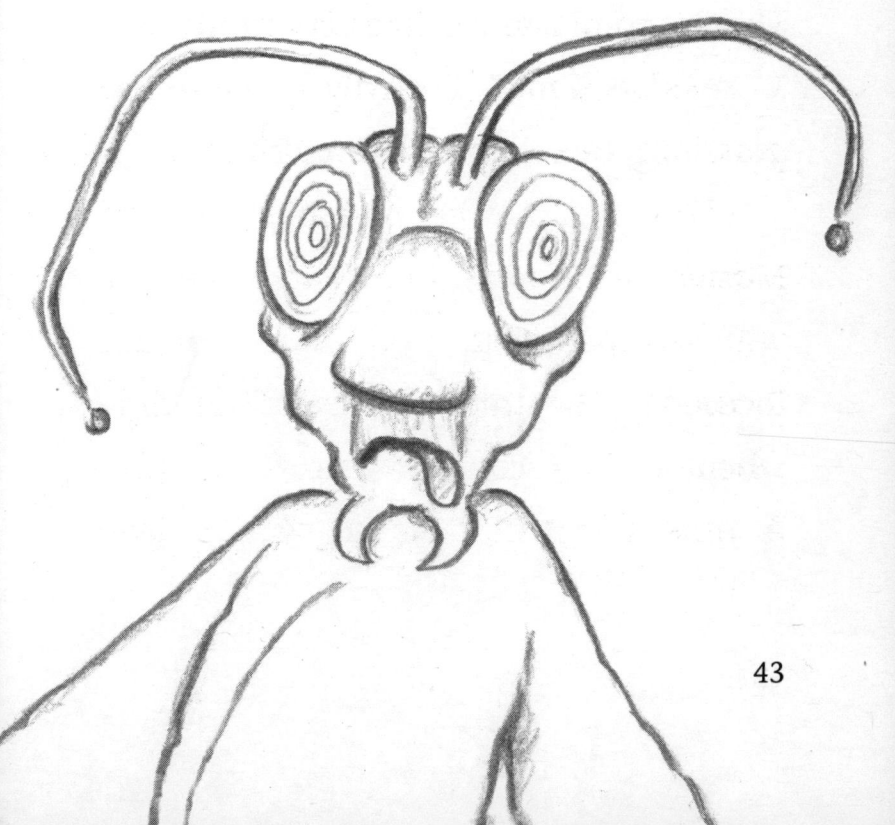

'Master!' Superfly called, running over to his old tutor.

But Grand Master was having another vision. His head rolled. 'No . . . no!' he wailed. His fragile body shook. 'NOOOOOO!'

Grand Master floated up off the floor. 'Cannot! Will not!' Then, with a croaking 'Nooooo!', he collapsed in Superfly's arms.

The room fell silent.

Just as Midge was about to give him the kiss of life, the old bug sat back up. 'You must beware!' he gasped.

'Love,' he wheezed.

'Trap,' he spluttered.

Then, with wild eyes, he shouted,

'DANGER!'

And I'm Rose Baumer, with the head lice – er, I mean headlines. The owner of a top Bugville store has been held captive whilst his fancy-dress-hire store was cleared of wigs, clown suits and rain-coats. Fly News reporter Freya Lemar is live at the scene . . .

That's right, Rose. Last night, Winston Turnbull heard strange noises in his store. When he went to investigate, he was forced into a pink tutu and sombrero and left locked in a changing room whilst the store was ransacked. Mr Turnbull remains in a state of shock. Reporting for Fly News, this is Freya Lemar.

Chapter 6
BUGVILLE BRIDGE

It was the afternoon of the TV awards ceremony and, besides the Turnbull's robbery, all was quiet in Bugville. Superfly and Midge had left Grand Master sleeping, and were sitting by the river, thinking about the old grasshopper's 'vision'.

Quietly they watched Bugville Bridge raising its two halves to allow boats through, before they were lowered and traffic thundered across them again.

Feeling a little drowsy, Bugville's heroes closed their eyes, until . . .

'Oh Holy Moly!' a passing lady-bug yelled, pointing at Bugville Bridge. 'Look!'

One half of the bridge had gone up again before the traffic had stopped, leaving a school bus teetering dangerously over the edge!

The heroes kicked their turbo boots into action and . . .

'S-U-P-E-R FLY!'
and 'M-I-D-G-E!'

. . . came ripping across the sky.

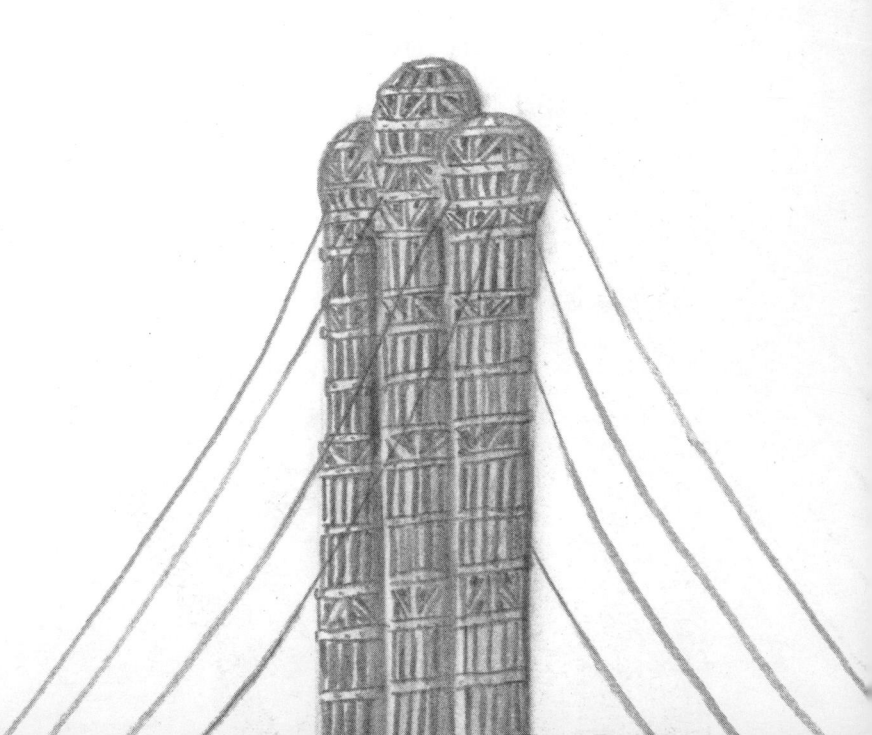

'There must be a fault with the bridge's electrical system,' Superfly shouted.

He was right. A lightning bolt had hit the engine room and caused the bridge to lift without stopping the traffic first. But where had the lightning come from? It wasn't even raining.

Before Midge could check, a big gust of wind blew, tipping the school bus further over the raised edge.

'Hey, that's Sister Aphid, the teacher from my niece's school!' Superfly said, hovering close to the bus.

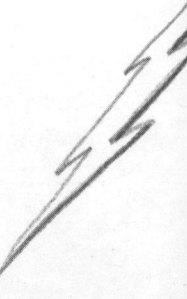

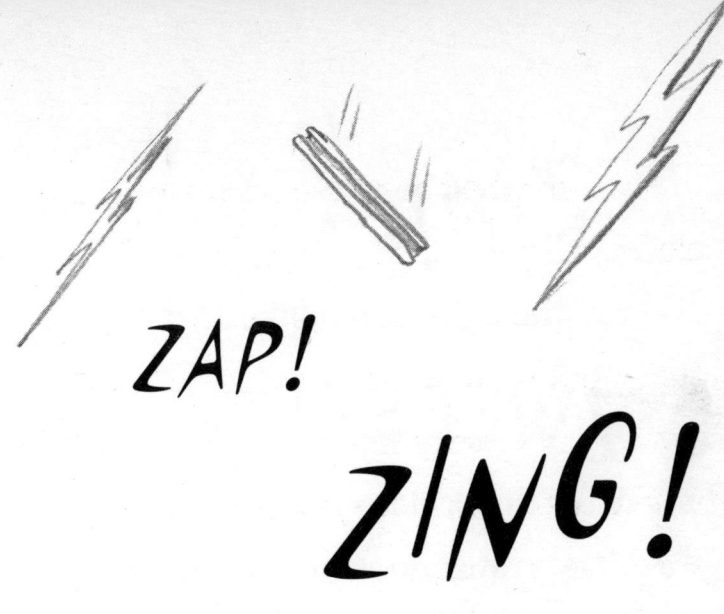

ZAP!

ZING!

Suddenly, lightning bolts tore past them in the sky. Superfly reached for his weapons belt to pull out his laser-wing boomerang but . . .

Watch out below!

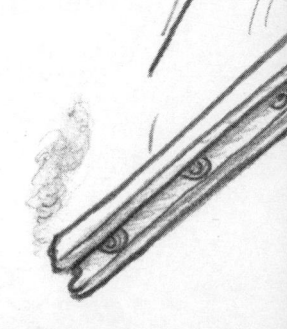

ZiP!

. . . the lightning bolts . . .

ZWEEEE! . . . kept coming.

Now the bridge was being hit.

The crowd looked up and gasped. First at the falling girders about to crush them. Then at Midge . . .

. . . who was catching girders and throwing them into the river!

Midge whistled to Superfly.

'Not now, Midge!' his hovering partner shouted as he stared down into the crowd. 'I'm using my extra-sensory vision

to see where the lightning's coming from.
Though I think I know *exactly* who it is.'

Poor Midge. He was only trying to tell
his partner to look out . . .

. . . for the bus!

The lightning bolts had broken some of the supports that held the bridge, making it jerk and fling the bus into the air. The wind bounced it up and down, tumbling the aphids around inside. Superfly needed to do something – fast!

Suddenly, the wind dropped.

Superfly landed on the bridge's lowered half and gazed up.

The bus was hurtling, headfirst, towards him! Superfly closed his eyes and raised his arms. The hero's heart pounded. He gulped and then . . . *then*

. . . THEN!

Chapter 7

ELECTRIFLIED!

Who would've believed it? Without even touching it, Superfly was holding a school bus above his head. Wow! How did he do that?

Midge. Ah, yes, Midge. Overlooked, as usual.

He was holding the bus in mid-air. It was Midge who'd saved the bus full of aphids.

He kept the school bus hovering long enough to let the young aphids jump out.

'Bless you, dear fly,' Sister Aphid called to Superfly. 'Everyone is safe now, thank you.'

Superfly moved out of the way, just as . . .

CRASH!

Midge let go of the bus.

'Hey, Midge. Where ya been, buddy?' Superfly said. 'You missed all the action.'

Midge rolled his eyes, then, suddenly, he started hissing.

'What is it, Midge?' Superfly asked.

A buzzing sound was coming from behind him. *Is that Bruno 'Bruiser' Bee?* he thought. Then . . .

BUUUUUURRRPPP!

. . . a disgusting belch gave it away.

It was his old enemy **Electro Slug**!

'That was very rude,' Sister Aphid announced.

I knew it!

'Oh, I know, Sister,' Electro Slug mocked. 'But then, so is THIS!'

A lightning bolt hit Sister Aphid smack between the eyes. She'd been electriflied!

The crowd gasped in horror. Then a couple of her young aphids whooped for joy.

'Now, you,' said Electro Slug, turning to Superfly. 'Look at me when I'm talking to you!'

The hero was fumbling with a gadget on his belt.

Electro Slug raised his arms. He flared his eyes. He curled his top lip. Then . . . he started smacking himself on the head.

'Ow! I'm being bitten to death by that ridiculous midge!'

Suddenly, a moped pulled up. Electro Slug slimed on the back and leaned towards Superfly. 'I haven't finished with you yet,' he hissed.

The moped sped away, leaving Superfly wondering about its driver.

Boy, that really looked like Freya Lemar, he thought.

Sister Aphid started to recover and reporters gathered round Superfly. But he noticed his favourite was missing.

Could that have been Freya Lemar driving? he wondered again.

Superfly's antennae started to vibrate. His phone was ringing. It was Grand Master.

'I've had that vision again, young one,' the old bug sighed. 'Same thing. Beware – love, trap . . . *danger.*'

But Superfly wasn't listening. Only one thing was on his mind: *What was Freya Lemar doing on a moped with that bad boy, Electro Slug?*

Chapter 8
BELLE'S BEAUTY BAR

Well, of course, it wasn't really Freya Lemar on that moped. It was Loo, the waiter from Scrappy Burgers. The fan in Fancy's Department Store who got her autograph, remember?

Anyway, the real Freya Lemar was in Belle's Beauty Bar with Melba Modem. Her good friend was treating her to some pampering before the Bugville TV Awards later on.

There she was, wearing – oo-er! – just a couple of towels! She'd had a wing massage, her legs waxed and false nails put on. Now she was wearing a face-pack, enjoying the peace. Or trying to, but Melba was talking.

'Well, anyways, I told him that's no way to treat a lady. Hey! What about the Bugville TV Awards tonight, honey? D'ya think Superfly'll be there?'

'Mmmmm . . .' Freya replied, careful not to crack her face-pack.

A beauty therapist came in.

Freya hoped Superfly *would* be at the ceremony. She pictured him giving her an award, punching a hole in the ceiling with his mega-catapult, then flying her to a beautiful spot overlooking the city. They'd loop the loop together, they'd beat bad bugs together, they'd –

RRRRRIIIPPPPPP! The therapist tore wax strips off Melba's legs.

'AAAAAAAARRRRRRGGGGGHHHH!!!!!!'

Melba's cry interrupted Freya's dream. 'So, are you gonna ask that cute Superfly for an exclusive interview?' she asked, rubbing her leg. 'You know – "Inside the Secret World of Superfly".'

But before Freya could answer, the music on the TV suddenly stopped.

'Oh great. Just what we need,' Melba said. 'A news flash!'

Fly News

We interrupt this programme again to bring you some more breaking news. I'm Ed Baxter.

'Woah! I can't believe it!' Melba blurted. 'That was those creepy fans I saw you with in Fancy's! And why's the little one dressed up like you?'

Freya grabbed her phone as Melba gathered their things.

'That's it! I'm going to the Police Station to clear my name,' the reporter said, turning her phone on.

Halfway through listening to her voicemail – all messages from the police – she burst into tears.

'Oh honey, I know,' Melba said, rushing over. 'What's worse? An expensive face-mask cracking so easily or being mistaken for a lowdown creep?'

Freya paused. Melba had a point. How could anyone mistake her for such a hideously ugly look a like? It didn't make sense.

Poor Freya sobbed on Melba's shoulder. Then she let out the loudest scream ever heard in Belle's Beauty Bar. They were used to hearing LOUD screams, but this one was

LOUDER!

Chapter 9

THE SECRET HIDE-OUT

Now, even though Superfly and Midge had cleaned Bugville up, there were still a few dirty corners left in the city. Like the one with this old, abandoned warehouse in it.

Well, *inside* this old, abandoned warehouse was a secret hide-out – the hide-out of a certain slug and a woodlouse,

who were standing at the top of the stairs, in front of a locked broom-cupboard.

'He still say nothing, Electro,' said Loo.

'And you've tried . . . everything?'

'Everything,' sighed Loo, jangling his keys.

'Even . . . THIS?'

'A feather duster?' Loo scoffed. He put a key in the door.

'No,' Electro corrected him. 'It's a tickling stick.'

'No, no. It a feather duster.'

'Tickling stick.'

'Feather.'

'Tickling.'

'Feather. Oh, stick it!' Loo snapped, opening the door.

CRRREEEEEEEEEEEEEEEEEKKKK!

Electro Slug studied the bound beetle in the broom-cupboard.

'You want me to clean him with this?' Loo teased, waving the feather duster under Electro Slug's triple chin.

'Pah!' spat the slug. 'How can he talk with this sticky plaster over his mouth!'

RRRRRIIIIIIIIIIIIIIIIIIPPPPP!

Poor Monty De Larentis – Bugville's

new Chief of Police. Left in a cupboard for hours. No wonder he smelt bad. Loo twirled the feathery stick along the Chief's sides.

'Tee-hee. Hee-hee,' the beetle tittered. How humiliating.

'Get up!' Electro Slug ordered. 'Take him to the rooftop,' the slug barked at Loo. 'I'll make him talk there.'

The Police Chief clambered up some stairs.

'Faster!' Loo snapped, prodding the Chief's bottom with the feather duster.

Then, even on the rooftop, things didn't get any easier for him . . .

'What's the security code to get backstage at the Bugville TV Awards?' Electro Slug bellowed at the Chief, firing sparks at his feet.

'What time will Superfly arrive?'

PED-OWW!

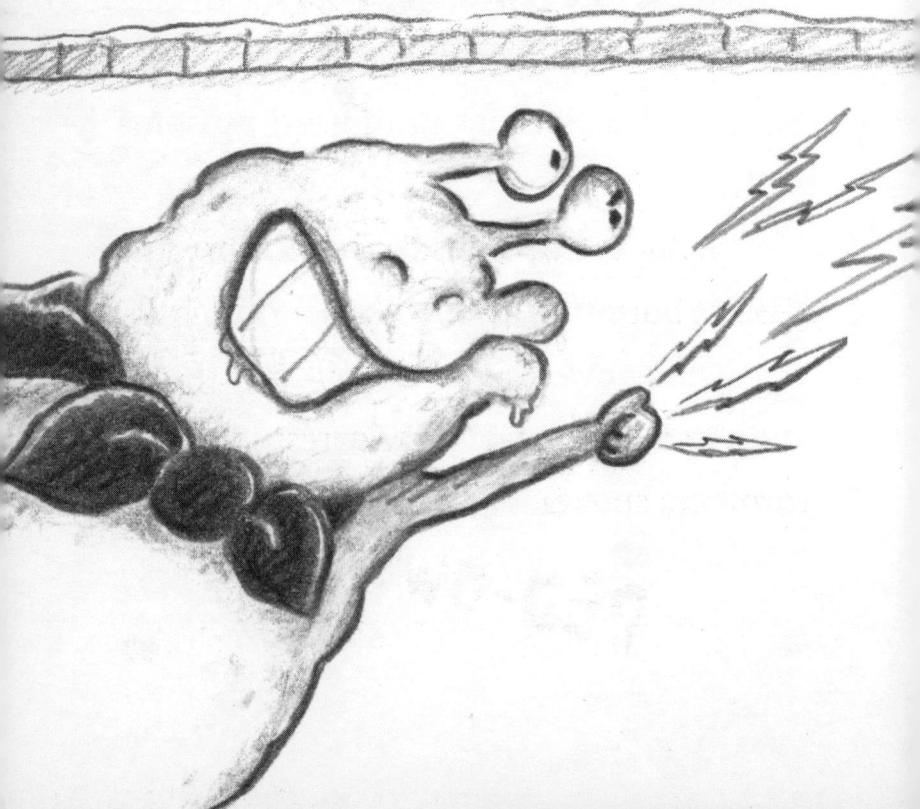

'What's the world record for the loudest burp?' **FIZZ-OWW!**

'And why did you arrest me for throwing snowballs at you last month?'

PED-OWW!

Meanwhile, downstairs, Loo was copying something that was written on a notepad, then dropping his used pieces of paper on the floor. What a litter-bug!

'Yes!' he cried at last. He'd copied the words perfectly.

He took a card out from his drawer and scribbled the same words at the

THE 56TH ANNUAL
Bugville TV Awards
V.I.B. PASS • ACCESS ALL AREAS
Freya Lemar

bottom. Why, that greasy louse had made a fake backstage pass to the Bugville TV Awards! He's such a cheater!

And what had he been copying over and over?

Freya Lemar? Freya Lemar! Why, that smelly louse had been copying her autograph – the one she'd given him and Electro Slug in Fancy's Department Store.

Loo got up and stared at the collection of his favourite things. There, on the wall, among the photos, cutouts, bus tickets and out-of-date party invites, was a picture of the lovely reporter.

'Soon, Fly-girl,' the creep sighed, before he planted a sloppy kiss on Freya Lemar's nose. Yuck! How gross!

Loo pulled on a raincoat and plonked a blonde wig on his head. Oh no, the master of disguise was at it again!

Having finished admiring himself, Loo sat back at his computer to find out some more details about the upcoming Awards ceremony . . .

Only Bugville's Police Chief knows all the security codes, times and plans for the 56th Annual Bugville TV Awards. All backstage passes must be signed by the holder and authorised by the chief's official stamp — no stamp, no entry!

'Hmmm. So we need stamp, eh?' Loo said, picking up his fake pass. 'To the rooftop! Quick!'

Chapter 10

EMPTY POCKETS

Up on the roof of the warehouse, Electro Slug was still firing questions at the Police Chief. Only now the Chief was on a flagpole, high over the street. One more flash of Electro Slug's lightning bolts and the flagpole would be frazzled and the Chief would fall to his death! Electro Slug raised his arms and . . .

'WAIT!' Loo shouted.

Electro Slug lowered his arms again. 'Stamp this pass with your special stamp,' Loo said, thrusting his fake pass at the Police Chief.

But still, the Chief said and did nothing.

'Untie him and hook him up by his feet!' Electro Slug ordered, pointing to a crane behind them.

Loo obeyed, then watched the Police Chief dangle upside down in the air.

Poor Chiefy – after all he'd been through he still hadn't told them anything about the Bugville TV Awards!

'Shaky him up and down!' Loo shouted, lifting the lid off a packing crate to catch everything that fell out of the Chief's pockets:

A rubber bone . . . a mobile phone . . . a Scrappy Burgers Loyalty card . . . a missing piece to someone's jigsaw puzzle . . . the seating plan for the 56th Annual Bugville TV Awards . . . some fizzy cola bottles . . . a whistle . . . keys . . . a string of plastic sausages . . . the timetable for the 56th Annual Bugville TV Awards . . . a portable ink pad for taking fingerprints . . . a plunger . . . bubble-gum . . . an 'Authorised by Bugville

Police Department' rubber stamp . . . and a plug for the kitchen sink.

Loo took what he needed and stamped his pass.

'You'll never get away with it,' the Chief slurred, speaking at last. 'You'll never fool anyone with that disguise. You're way too ugly to pass for Freya Lemar.'

Loo threw the Chief's phone to Electro Slug.

'Ha!' cried the slug, listening to the Chief's voicemail. 'But your little disguise *did* fool the cops, Loo – they've caught Freya Lemar!'

Electro Slug paused. 'But wait, this could backfire. If they throw Freya Lemar in jail, our plan will be ruined! Unless . . . I'm just going to make a few calls.

Call One: the Police Station.

Bugville Police Department.

Yeah, it's the Chief here.

Hey Chief – where ya been? Some pretty bad things've been goin' on.

Uh – I got some kinda bad bug. (cough)

Huh. That Fly News reporter, Freya Lemar's here – the one suspected of robbing Turnbull's and causing trouble on Bugville Bridge. You wanna question her?'

Nope. She has to be at the Bugville TV Awards tonight. Let her go. (sniff)

Er, OK, Chief. I'll go tell her now.

Call Two: Freya Lemar.

Hello, Freya Lemar speaking.

Bugville's Police Chief here, Miss Lemar. My officers have made a huge mistake, so please have a Special Backstage Pass to tonight's TV Awards on me.
You never know, you might meet Superfly there.

Why, that's —

The least I can do, Miss Lemar. Collect your pass at the stage door at seven-thirty. Sharp.

Thank you. See you there!

Freya Lemar fell for it – hook, line and stinker!

Now what were those creeps up to? Why did they need Freya Lemar to be backstage at the Bugville TV Awards?

The reporter rushed out of the police station with Melba and headed home. Home to powder her nose and grab a bite to eat. Home to sing in the shower and get dressed to the nines.

Home, sweet home – the wonderful place she'd soon be wishing she'd never left at all.

Chapter 11
A POOL OF SLIME

At last it was time for the glamour, excitement and SURPRISE of the 56th Annual Bugville TV Awards.

Superfly had ironed his suit.

Midge had polished his teeth.

There seemed to be only one bug in town not getting ready to watch the show – the Police Chief. Left clinging to the warehouse flagpole, all he could watch was Loo's moped speeding away.

Over at the red carpet, meanwhile, the crowds were busy star-spotting. There was the show's host, Jonathan Moth. There was Stag Taggart, the wrestler.

There was long-jumper Dusty Ricketts with Tim Zip, the fastest beetle in Bugville! There by the steps were Superfly and Midge, signing autographs and posing for pictures. And there, behind them, was someone in a real hurry.

'Freya Lemar?' The backstage security guard asked. He studied the fake pass. 'You're shorter than you look on TV. Sign here, please.'

Loo – who it really was of course –

waited as the rhino beetle checked the signature against the one on the pass.

'That's fine,' the guard smiled, letting Loo stroll into the backstage area. 'Have a nice night, Miss Lemar.'

Loo passed tumbling ants and sitar-playing weevils – the entertainment for the evening – searching for Electro Slug. He passed two electriflied security bugs – Electro Slug was close by. Then . . .

'What took you so long?' Electro Slug snapped from behind him. 'That silly reporter will be here any minute.' The nervous slug snatched the fake pass from Loo. It was seven-thirty – sharp.

KNOCK! KNOCK! KNOCK!

Loo opened the stage door and Freya Lemar stepped inside. Then . . .

BANG!

He slammed the door shut behind her, leaving her face to face with Electro Slug.

'Looking for this?' Electro Slug asked, waving the fake backstage pass.

The news reporter gasped. 'Why, you're the two creeps I met in Fancy's! The robbers who tried to kill a bus full of aphids, pretending to be me!'

'Yeah, yeah, yeah, we bad,' Loo admitted. 'But we still big fan of you, remember?'

Freya lunged at the louse but slipped in a pool of slime, and slid headfirst into Electro Slug's big tummy.

The mean old slug sucked his stomach in, to stop her escaping. Her head was stuck. What a scoundrel!

Quickly Loo clipped her wings together with some clothes pegs so she couldn't fly away. Then, he pinned her arms by her waist and wrapped an old corset around her, so she couldn't move them. The real Freya Lemar could only kick her legs in the air, as the fake one pulled the corset strings tighter and tighter around her . . . Ouch!

'Where's Superfly and his amazing powers now?' the slug cackled. He let his huge stomach go, sending the news reporter flying. Double ouch!

In a flash, Loo rushed over and tied a silky scarf around her mouth. Tight. 'Sorry, lovely lady,' he whispered.

Freya Lemar stamped down on his foot. Hard. Triple ouch!

Chapter 12

AND THE WINNER IS...

While Electro Slug and Loo were kidnapping Freya backstage, Superfly and Midge were enjoying their night off, watching the show's opening performance – Stag Taggart wrestling his rival, the minotaur beetle, Cody Jones.

As Cody Jones was carried off stage, someone was still entering the hall. As the audience went wild for Stag Taggart, *someone* was finding their seat.

Someone?

'Hey, Freya. How ya been?' Superfly asked the someone taking their seat in front of him. But there was no answer. Embarrassed at being ignored, Superfly turned away to gulp his fizzy slime juice.

'What's up with Freya, Midge?' he whispered 'She usually says plenty.'

Midge looked over and frowned.

'Maybe she's lost her voice,' Superfly guessed. 'There are some bad bugs going round.'

Some shifty-looking beetles looked over at him. 'It's OK, guys . . . not you,' he said.

Meanwhile, Midge had started

bouncing on his fork, hissing and spitting through his teeth.

'You're right, Midge. Maybe she has changed. Maybe that really *was* her driving Electro Slug around today. Maybe she's not the fly I thought she was. Maybe . . .'

Midge had heard enough. He'd already seen through Loo's thin disguise, even if Superfly hadn't. He knew that spineless louse wasn't Freya Lemar. And he was going to do something about it!

As Superfly waffled on, Midge hovered behind the fake Freya. Then he started chomping through the raincoat's stitching. Loo swatted him away, and then . . .

CLONK!

Midge had been hit! He dropped down on to the table top. Quickly, Loo slammed a glass down over him. Midge was trapped!

Completely unaware of this, Superfly was taking a call.

'Yes, Grand Master. What is it?' he whispered into his phone.

'Beware, young one,' the old grasshopper warned. 'My vision . . .'

'Grand Master,' Superfly sighed. 'They're about to present the first award – I'll call you later.'

'And the award for best news reporter goes to . . .' Jonathan Moth paused. 'Freya Lemar from **Fly News**!'

The audience clapped and cheered. A spotlight followed Loo, the fake Freya, weaving his way between tables towards the stage. TV cameras zoomed in and out on him, looking for a flattering shot. Whispers spread through the audience, as Loo finally stepped on to the stage – and tripped.

Man, she got ugly!

Chapter 13

FROM SUPERFLY ...

As the fake Freya fell, off flew the blonde wig, landing in a dragonfly's soup. Then the fake Freya's raincoat ripped off – and revealed . . . the wingless back of – gasp! – a rotten woodlouse!

The place went wild! Stag Taggart hurled bread rolls at the stage. Tim Zip threw celery sticks. Melba Modem threw her left shoe. What a bun fight! What a fiasco!

Superfly zipped into the air and landed on stage in front of Loo, as Jonathan Moth tried calming things down with a few jokes.

Suddenly, sparks showered everywhere – Electro Slug had slithered on stage!

'**BURP!**' The slug picked up Jonathan Moth's microphone, as everyone stared in horror. Everyone, that is, except Loo. The woodlouse escaped behind the curtain.

'I am Electro Slug!' Loo's fizzing friend announced. 'Remember me? Ha ha ha ha ha ha!' Sparks flew out of the speakers.

'And the Bugville TV Award for most tempting bait goes to . . .' Electro Slug paused dramatically.

Loo tilted a spotlight towards the dark ceiling.

'The *real* Freya Lemar!'

The audience gasped. There she was, Freya Lemar – a Bugville TV Award winner – bound and gagged and balancing on a high beam.

Superfly flew into the air and back-flipped over the flying sparks. 'OK, Electro,' he yelled. 'We've heard enough. Take this!'

ZWEEEEEE!  BAM!

Superfly's rocket boomerang was shot down in flames by one of Electro Slug's electric zaps.

'Right, Slug-face,' Superfly cried. 'Get a loada this!'

His triple quick-fire peashooter was fried.

'You've no chance against this, slime ball!' Superfly shouted.

ZWING!

His mega whirly-gig was put out of action.

With an empty weapons belt, a scorched suit and a missing partner, things were not looking good for Superfly.

Then . . .

ZIPPAH!

Superfly
was hit
by a sizzler!
The hero
dropped
like,
well,
a fly.

Freya let out a loud, muffled scream. The audience let out an even louder groan. No, things really weren't looking good . . .

'Well, well, well,' Electro Slug fizzed, sliming over to the fallen hero. 'Superfly – at last you're all mine.' The slug raised his arms and cackled. 'Now,' he said. 'Get ready to face your –'

'WAIT!' a voice cried.

'Oh, what NOW?' Electro Slug snapped.

'We play game, Electro,' Loo said. 'Remember?' He waved a gaudy, ruffley-collared clown suit in the slug's face.

'Put silly suit on – quick!' Loo ordered Superfly.

The superhero giddily stepped into the suit.

'Come on, come on. Get on with it!' Electro Slug barked, as Loo scurried off behind the curtain. Poor Superfly. He was still in a daze. Loo returned to the stage, driving the crane they had used earlier on the roof. But, why had they brought it to the awards ceremony? Suddenly, he abandoned the crane and scampered off again.

'You can't leave that crane there – it's dangerous!' an old ladybug shouted after him. 'Someone could get their foot caught in that chain!'

She was right. The chain was lying all over the stage.

'Hey, look!' a stink bug called, pointing at Superfly back-flipping across the stage. 'Superfly's recovered!'

'Go, Superfly, go!' everyone cheered.

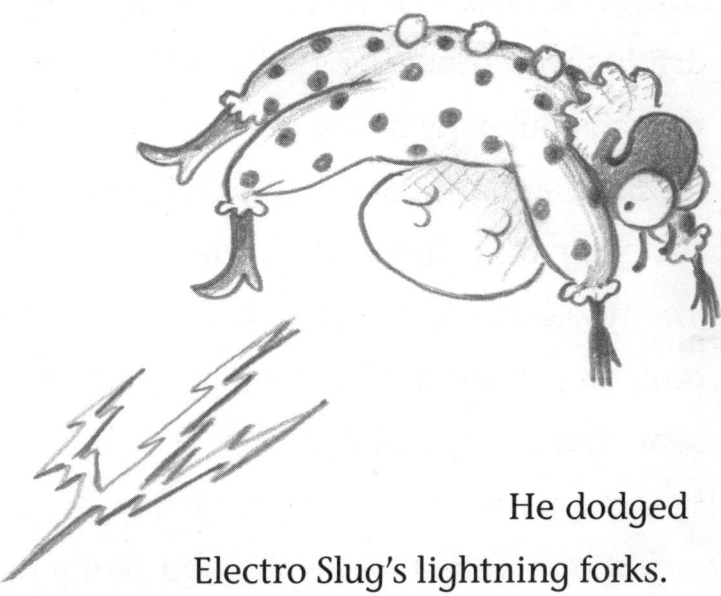

He dodged Electro Slug's lightning forks.

'Go, Superfly, go!'

He spun a triple backward 360°.

'Go, Superfly . . .'

But then his foot got caught in the chain. Didn't that ladybug say it was dangerous? Worse still, the chain was moving. And tightening around Superfly's leg!

Bugville's hero struggled.

'No, Superfly, no!' the audience yelled.

Bugville's hero was dragged across the stage.

'No, Superfly, no!' the audience groaned.

Bugville's hero was hoisted up. Up, up, up . . . until Superfly was left hanging upside down over a packing crate.

A crate full of starving baby spiders!

Yuck!

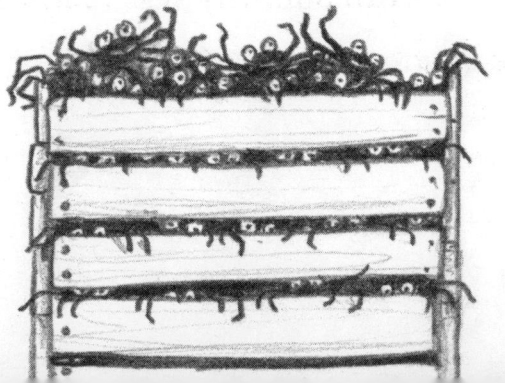

Chapter 14

...TO SUPERCLOWN

'Ha! Ha! Look at you!' Electro Slug shot out blue sparks with glee. 'A silly little fly dressed as a clown. Ner-ner-ne-ner-ner!'

Electro Slug stared into the TV camera. 'Now,' he began. 'All you flies will see how it feels to be laughed at. To be made fun of. To be humiliated.'

A silverfish wiped a tear from her eye.

'And now,' the slug continued, 'this

pathetic fly will be lowered into this crate of starving spiderlings, suffering a slow, painful death! All because of you flies!'

The slug leaned over the crate. 'But before we wave bye-bye, let's allow "Super Clown" to say a few last words. A little . . . catchphrase, perhaps?' he teased. 'How about those three ridiculous little words? They always make *me* laugh . . .'

'Midge!' Superfly yelled desperately.

'Midge?' Electro Slug scoffed. 'Ha! Midge is a joke! Come on now – make us laugh, Super Clown.'

Loo started lowering Superfly into the crate.

Superfly really was in a pickle. No Midge, Freya stuck on a high beam, plus he was unable to kick his turbo boots into action, and was being lowered into a crate of spiders. Was this really going to be the end of Superfly?

The deflated hero started dropping slowly. Excited spiderlings clambered up the sides of the crate to watch their dinner coming towards them.

Suddenly, Superfly thought of something. It was a long shot, but it just might work.

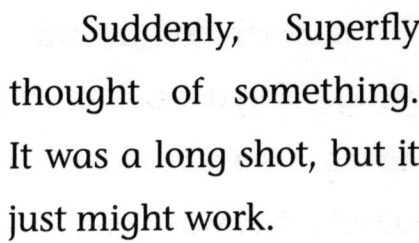

What goes 'Aaaaa–poooooo?' A slug with a cold!

The audience were silent. Until . . .

Some bed bugs sniggered on table seven. The fleas on table nine tittered. Several goth moths even smirked. Then, before long, the entire place was filled with laughter.

Electro Slug was sizzling mad. 'Stop it! Stop it!' he yelled. Painful memories

of being mocked by flies came flooding back. A time when flies would land on him, mistaking him for a fat, juicy poo. A time he'd rather forget.

Electro Slug turned blue with rage as sparks showered out of him. He was about to blow a fuse!

His electrical power surged . . .

'WAAAAAAARG

. . . and blew every light in the house – leaving the Bugville TV Awards in complete . . .

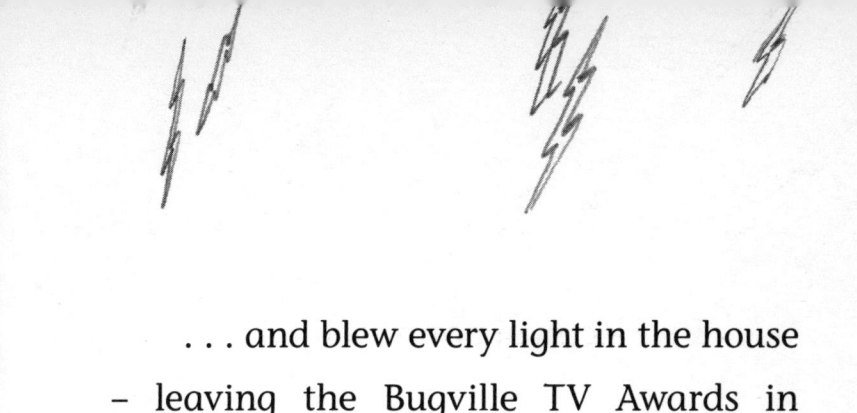

. . . DARKNESS!!

OUCH!
Oooof!
FIZZZZZ
SOCK!
Where've you been, Midge?
AAAaaaRGHH!
NOOOOOO!!
POW!

ZAP! ZING!
Ta-dah!
BURP!
RRRIIIPPP!
CHOMP! CHOMP! CHOMP!
Mind your manners, honey
PAH!
GET OFF MY FOOT!
Hey, fireflies! Turn on your lights!

Chapter 15
PIECE O' CAKE!

Suddenly, hundreds of fireflies lit the place up, revealing all.

Midge, who Loo had trapped under a glass, was now hovering over the stage. He'd eaten through the table top, flown over to Superfly and bitten through the chain to set his friend free.

Electro Slug was hanging from the chain now, with spiderlings swinging off his tail.

Loo was pinned to a table top with Melba's right shoe stuck firmly on his head.

Superfly and Freya Lemar were flying down from the high beam, about to follow some miming mantids to the emergency exit. Not quite punching a hole in the roof like she'd imagined, but still a rescue!

And finally, there was Melba Modem, barefoot and carefree, getting Stag Taggart to give her a piggy-back through the fleeing crowds.

Once outside, Midge, the little gentleman, chomped through Freya's moth-eaten corset.

'How'd that louse get it so tight, honey?' Melba asked. 'I mean, look at your waist – it's like a wasp's!'

Freya couldn't answer. Not until . . . 'Aaaah . . . I can breathe again,' she sighed. 'Thank you, Midge! You're SO adorable.'

'Adorable? Did you see Stag Taggart droppin' me out here?' Melba gushed.

'Now, that's adorable, honey.'

But Freya wasn't listening. She was too busy gazing into Superfly's eyes, thanking him, before asking him for an e x c l u s i v e interview that would reveal everything about Bugville's favourite superheroes.

'Ow!' Superfly yelped. Midge didn't like interviews, so he'd given his friend a little bite to make sure he'd say no.

'Where is he? Where is that sparking

slug?' a voice said behind them. 'I'm gonna fry him in a salt stack and feed him to some chickens!'

It was the Police Chief. He'd finally wriggled free and walked miles to warn everyone of Electro Slug's plan. Obviously, he was too late.

'The slime ball's still hanging out inside,' Superfly joked. 'Listen!'

Wooo! Stop it! **BURP!** Ha, ha! That tickles!

'Sounds like the spiderlings are on to him too,' Superfly said. 'What d'ya say, Midge?'

'Hee-hee-hee,' his tiny pal sniggered, 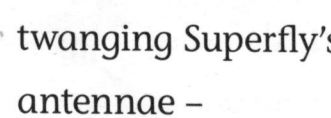 twanging Superfly's antennae –

BOING!

Bugville's news reporters ran over to hear how Superfly had managed to save the day at the last minute, when suddenly Midge started poking him in his side.

'Gimme a minute, flies,' Superfly said, stepping aside. 'Midge! What is it, buddy?'

Midge pointed at the waiting crowds. They needed Superfly to shout the three little words that told them Bugville was safe once again.

The hero took a deep breath.

He leaned back.

Then he shouted . . .

And so, as fireworks lit up the sky, and Bugville partied, we can only ask: Who would've known so much would go on at the Bugville TV Awards? Who would've thought mistaking a slug for a poo would make them go crazy? Who would have believed Superfly would be in danger because of Freya Lemar? Who? Grand Master Grasshopper, that's who.

I've had a vision . . .

Wow! It's Grand Master! And it sounds like he's talking to *you*!

There is more to come. More high—kicking villains . . .

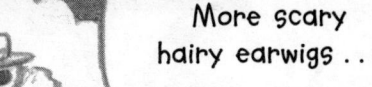

'DANGER!'

Uh-oh! 'Till next time, bug lovers!